T0131946

Big Rig
rescues
Santa

written by
Nita McFarlin

To order additional copies of this book, contact:
Xlibris
1-888-795-4274
www.Xlibris.com
Orders@Xlibris.com

The radio in the big truck crackled with static! Tom, the driver, twisted and turned the knobs until he could understand the voice of the announcer. "We seem to have lost Santa and his reindeer on our radar screen", the late night host stated excitedly!

Then silence again as the connection was lost.

Tom was one of numerous long distance truck drivers delivering freight all over America. He loved his job, loved knowing he helped deliver important merchandise to businesses everywhere.

Tom was on his way home, it was Christmas eve, he had delivered his last load and was hoping to be in bed before Santa came to visit!

The purr of his big motor and the warmth of his cab were comforting as he peered out the snowy window.

"Santa lost on the radar? What could have happened to him?" Maybe something is wrong with the radar. Santa never gets lost, he'll show up, I know he will, he always does.

Around a curve on the mountainous highway Tom could see swaying pine and cedar trees, powdery snow blowing from their sparkling needles. The wind was whipping around and the snow was thicker than he had seen before, great mounds accumulating, lucky for Tom his truck was equipped to handle these situations. He was proud of his tough vehicle, proud the company he worked for provided him with a truck streamlined and classy, powerful with an up-to-date chassis.

"Come on Big Rig, come on", he heard on his CB radio! Tom's handle, the name he was known by to the other truckers was Big Rig, all the truckers had their own unique handle identifying them to their fellow truckers. "Go ahead", Tom answered.

"Hey Big Rig, this is the Rambler", came the reply. Did you hear the news, Santa Claus is lost on the radar screen? "Yep, I heard", Tom answered, "but I think there must be a mistake. Santa never gets lost, must be something wrong with the radar screen!"

"Hope so, Big Rig, hope so! Don't know what would happen if Santa is lost! Christmas wouldn't be Christmas if Santa didn't come! We'll keep our eyes and ears open, see you when we get to the terminal!", Came the reply. "Ten four, Rambler, ten four", Tom replied and tried again unsuccessfully to get his radio to work.

Tom cracked his window for a breath of the fresh wintery air, pulled the collar of his coat up around his neck and made what he thought would be the last turn on the highway home. Little did he know what awaited him just around the next curve of the snowy mountain!

Santa Claus kissed Mrs. Claus Christmas eve, had the elves fill the sleigh with sugarplums, many different goodies, gifts, toys and his "been good list"! The reindeer were hitched in their usual fashion! He felt great, everything was running as planned, this Christmas eve was going to run like clock work,...Or so he thought.

They were off, all over the earth, spreading gifts and cheer! They were traveling in their old fashioned sleigh, pulled by Santa's trusty eight reindeer!

Santa felt a sense of accomplishment and jokingly sang as he, the sleigh and reindeer neared the end of their journey!

"We've seen Nebraska, Alaska, Wichita, Arkansas,... All of the countries you can find on your map, all of the villages, the towns and the cities, all of the earth! We've fullfilled wishes, spreading Christmas cheer and mirth!"

"This has been a record setting trip, we will be home early this year,..I can't wait to sit down with Mrs. Claus and have a cup of hot chocolate and some of the homemade cookies and candy I found left by the trees tonight! The reindeer and elves did a superb job this year and they will be richly rewarded, a big festive dinner with bonuses, food, music, lots of hay!", Santa cheerfully shouted to the reindeer!

Santa climbed down the chimney of a little mountain cabin. It looked almost like a brown gingerbread house with white snow frosting. The reindeer and sleigh were perched precariously on top. He placed toys beneath the little cedar tree lovingly decorated with popcorn garland, candy canes and hand made ornaments. Finished he gingerly climbed up, up, up and jumped into the sleigh!

All of a sudden when what did appear but a cascading avalanche on the sleigh and the deer!

The sleigh toppled over, the toys toppled out, the deer toppled and tangled and rolled all about!

"Where are you Dasher, Dancer, Vixen? What happened Prancer, Cupid, Comet, Donder, Blitzen?"

The snorting, the tugging, the jingling of bells filled the air with sounds the windy, wintry night carried around and over the mountain and into the open window of Big Rig's truck!

"What on earth, what can that be?" Tom asked himself as he lowered the window, slowed the engine and crept slowly around the curve on the slippery mountain highway the tires crunching on the snow as they turned.

A tumbling, a rumbling, a flashing of red, it appeared something was crashing, smashing on the road just ahead!

Tom moved even closer careful not to frighten the bundle of legs, noses, and ears protruding from the avalanche of snow that kept shifting around. Suddenly a fat little belly showed itself and the rest of Santa's body became recognizable as he rolled out and onto the road.

Santa brushed the snow off his coat, off his beard off his nose, he looked straight at Tom, from the snow he arose!

Tom slowed the big rig, pulled over, put his boot on the brake pedal, unfastened his seat belt, opened the door and stepped down into the white glistening outside world. He could not believe his eyes or his ears, could he be dreaming or was that Santa and the missing reindeer!

"Merry christmas Tom, I know you!", Santa said happily! "You live in the village below, the last stop on our trip. We were on our way to visit when we were delayed by that avalanche of snow! Now the reindeer are all in a tangle, the sleigh overturned, the toys and gifts need retrieving, my "been good" list is missing I have no time to burn!"

"Santa don't you worry, don't you fret! I have a big truck parked below, you'll make your deliveries yet!"

Tom and Santa coaxed the reindeer to stand up, to crawl out, they gathered sugarplums, toys, gifts that were scattered.

"Come on fellas", Tom shouted to the reindeer. "Let's get everything loaded in my truck, I'll give you a lift, we'll give the sleigh a good checking over at my work place, Santa can e-mail Mrs. Santa and have a new "been good list" faxed to him!"

"You'll make your last deliveries and be on your way, home, home, home, to the North Pole!"

"You know Tom," Santa laughed merrily as they finished their loading, "I always wanted to drive a big truck, how 'bout I give it a try?"

"Sure Santa," Tom answered, "But remember it won't fly, it runs on diesel fuel, not pulled by hooves going clippety-clop and you have a steering wheel not reins, sure Santa, give it a try!"

Off they went, down the mountain highway, down, down, down to the last village, down to deliver Christmas cheer on Santa's last been good list!

The mechanics at the company where Tom was employed gave the sleigh a good going over while Santa contacted Mrs. Santa for a new "been good list"! All damage repaired the sleigh was given a "go ahead"! Everyone clapped as Santa entered the shop to retrieve his vehicle and hitch the reindeer.

As he double checked the harness Santa gave Tom a big pat on the back and exclaimed, "Tom the world needs more people like you, people not afraid to get involved and give help to their fellowman, people who understand that giving is what christmas is all about, giving of yourself, of your time, remembering how much has been given to us, remembering the reason for this season! I will never forget what you and your co-workers did for me and the world tonight! You are definitely on my "been good list"!

Tom and his friends stood at the door as Santa in his old fashioned sleigh drawn by eight reindeer ascended into the velvety sky, stood in amazement as he shouted goodbye, their eyes wide with wonder, their hands cupped to their ear as they heard him exclaim,

"I'll see you next year!"

Printed in the United States
By Bookmasters